P9-DEL-603

SING WITH ME, LUCY MCGEE

SING WITH ME, LUCY MCGEE

BY

MARY AMATO

ILLUSTRATED BY JESSICA MESERVE

HOLIDAY HOUSE New York

Printed and bound in March 2019 at Maple Press, York, PA, USA.

First Edition

1 3 5 7 9 10 8 6 4 2

www.holidayhouse.com

Library of Congress Cataloging-in-Publication Data

Names: Amato, Mary, author. | Meserve, Jessica, illustrator.

Title: Sing with me, Lucy McGee / by Mary Amato; illustrated by Jessica Meserve.

Description: First edition. | New York: Holiday House, [2019] | Series: Lucy McGee; 2 | Summary: A talent contest brings out the worst in Lucy McGee and her fourth-grade classmates—Provided by publisher.

Identifiers: LCCN 2018015218 | ISBN 9780823438761 (hardcover)

Subjects: | CYAC: Behavior—Fiction. | Clubs—Fiction. | Talent shows—Fiction.

Classification: LCC PZ7.A49165 Sin 2019 | DDC [Fic]—dc23

LC record available at https://lccn.loc.gov/2018015218

For the next generation of duckies:
my grandnieces and grandnephews, Lilyana,
Adelyn, Joshua, Jack, Jett, Brooks, Grace,
Abby, and new baby Cahill

CONTENTS

Chapter One

SECRET GROUPS AND MONKEY TROOPS

My friend Phillip Lee walked up to me with a strange look on his face.

"Lucy," he whispered. "We need to spy."

We were having indoor recess because of rain, and I was in the Reading Corner of Mrs. Brock's room. Although the book I was reading about animals was

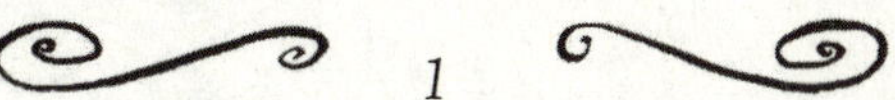

good, there is nothing like the word "spy" to grab your attention.

"Who are we spying on?" I asked.

"Scarlett. She's talking about the talent show," Phillip said.

Phillip took my book, and we crept over to the carpet near the cubbies and sat down. We pretended to look at the book, but we were spying. Scarlett and Victoria and Mara were talking on the other side of the cubby wall.

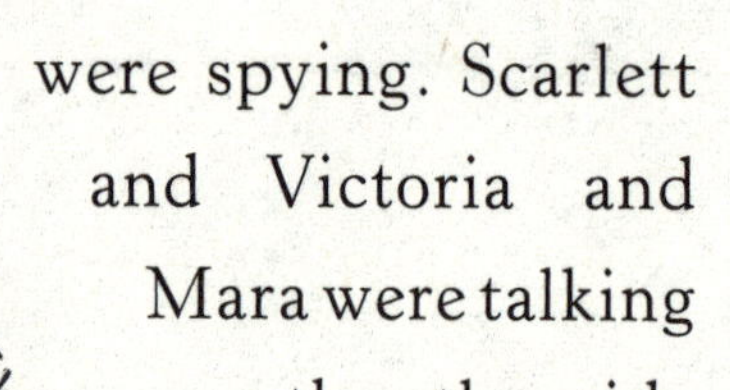

"Ms. Adamson said the talent show is for fourth and fifth graders only, which means it will be really good," Scarlett said. "Little kids would make it babyish."

"*So* babyish," Victoria said.

"I'm going to write a special song for us," Scarlett went on. "We'll be the best in the whole show."

"Is our group going to be just the three of us singing?" Mara asked. "Or all the fourth and fifth graders in the Songwriting Club?"

"Everybody except Lucy and Phillip," Scarlett said. "Don't tell them."

Phillip and I looked at each other. Scarlett wanted to leave us out?

"I'm going to write my song today," Scarlett whispered. "Let's have a secret group meeting tomorrow at recess to practice."

I couldn't believe it. A secret group without me and Phillip? That hurt.

Just then, Mrs. Brock walked by.

"What are you two doing?" she asked us.

"Just reading," I said quickly, looking down at the book.

The girls stopped talking, and Scarlett peeked out.

Phillip pointed to the open page. "Mrs. Brock, did you know that a group of monkeys is called a troop, and a group of dolphins is called a pod, and a group of lions is called a pride?"

"I did," Mrs. Brock said. "Animal group names are interesting. I'm glad you're enjoying that book."

Our teacher went to her desk, and Phillip and I raced back to the Reading Corner.

"We're all in the Songwriting Club

together," I said. "It isn't fair for Scarlett to leave us out. You're the one who started the club, Phillip."

"I know! And you're our best songwriter, Lucy," Phillip said. "The club should sing and play one of your songs at the show."

An idea popped into my head. "Let's try to write a great song," I said. "We can make it better than Scarlett's song. When everybody hears our song, they'll want to sing and play with us for the show."

Phillip smiled. "That's brilliant! We have to make it a catchy song. Everybody loves a catchy song."

"Let's do it right now!"

My heart started dancing with excitement. If you are wondering what that feels like, just imagine a troop of tiny monkeys having a party inside you.

The bell rang.

"Recess is over," Mrs. Brock said. "Clean up and get ready for math!"

Math?

The party was over. It felt like a herd of elephants had stomped in and chased the monkeys away!

Chapter Two

GO NUTS FOR DONUTS

Mrs. Brock started the math lesson with a warm-up word problem. "If a baker uses six cups of flour to make twelve blueberry donuts, twelve chocolate donuts, and twelve plain donuts, how many cups of flour would she need for each flavor? Write your answers down in your math

notebook. Remember, drawing a picture can help you solve your problem."

I raised my hand and Mrs. Brock came over to my desk.

"Mrs. Brock," I whispered. "Can I write a song instead of doing math?"

"No, Lucy," she whispered. "We're all doing math right now."

"Exactly," I said. "If everyone is doing math, then it wouldn't hurt if one person was writing a song."

"You can never have too many people doing math," she said. "Get to work."

Mrs. Brock loves math way too much.

I drew a picture of twelve plain donuts, twelve chocolate donuts, and twelve blueberry donuts. That's when it hit me. If a baker can make three different flavors of donuts at the

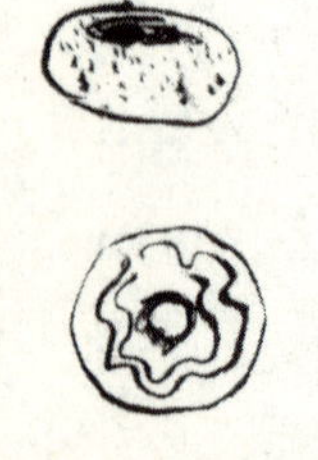

same time, I should be able to do math and write a song at the same time.

The first step: to write down all my ideas for songs.

Think. Think. Think.

Big problem! Three thinks + nothing = zero ideas.

I looked around the room. Sometimes I get ideas for songs by writing down things I see.

Ideas for Songs?

- Our class hamster chomping on a toilet paper roll
- The dirt on Resa's shoes
- Trash on the floor
- Raindrops rolling down the window

Oh no! Not good ideas!

"Lucy, get to work," Mrs. Brock said. "Pencil to the paper."

I looked at the donuts on my paper. If I ate 12 + 12 + 12 donuts, I bet my tooth would fall out. My tooth was loose, and I wanted it to fall out so I'd get money from the tooth fairy. I wiggled my tooth. It gave me an idea for a song!

I wrote:

Tooth, tooth, tooth
I wish you were dead.
I wish you would fall
Right out of my head.

Kind of catchy, right?

I looked up.

Scarlett was writing like crazy. Either she was doing the word problem or else she was writing her song. I had to know!

I raised my hand. "Mrs. Brock? Can I sharpen my pencil?"

"No, Lucy. You're wasting time. One more minute and then you need to turn your papers in."

Oh no! I looked down at the donuts on my paper. Then I wrote:

I go nuts for donuts.
Donuts are delicious.
I wish I had a dozen now—
They're tastier than fishes.

"Time's up," Mrs. Brock said. "Turn your papers in."

Mrs. Brock did not like my songs.

I had the same problem in science and social studies.

At the end of the day, Mrs. Brock gave me a letter to take home to my parents.

Dear Mr. and Mrs. McGee,

Lucy had a problem following directions. Her mind is wandering a lot. She is writing songs instead of doing her work. For homework, she needs to complete all the assignments that she should have done in class today.

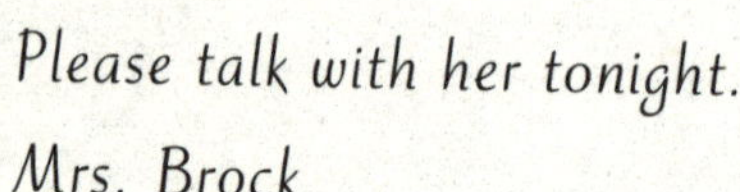

Please talk with her tonight.

Mrs. Brock

"Do you understand the problem, Lucy?" Mrs. Brock asked.

"I do," I said. "The problem is that it's hard to write a catchy song during school."

For some reason, Mrs. Brock gave me a little smile and asked, "What am I going to do with you, Lucy McGee?"

Chapter Three

QUACK ATTACK

I was supposed to show Mrs. Brock's letter to my dad after school. But when I got home, two wet, shiny ducks were in our bathtub!

"Quack, quack," said the small duck.

"Ack, Ack," said the smaller duck.

They weren't real ducks. They were my brother,

Leo, and my sister, Lily. Whenever Leo takes a bath, he turns into a duck or a seal or a shark. Or a puffer fish. But mostly a duck. And whatever Leo does, Lily copies. You could call her a copycat, but today you'd have to call her a copyduck.

"Hey Lucy!" My dad was sitting on the bathroom floor with his laptop. "Can you feed these two slippery-dippery ducks while I get dinner going?"

"I need to write a new song," I said. "There's a big talent show at school in twelve days, and Phillip and I want to sing in it with the Songwriting Club."

"That's great. But you can do it after dinner. I need help with these duckies." He was out the door before I could say anything about the letter from Mrs. Brock. So that part wasn't my fault.

I looked at Leo and Lily. "Dudes, I need to write a song!"

Leo smiled. "Me go—*quack*."

"Ha ha—*quack*," I said.

"Me hungry—*quack*," he said. Leo tucked his arms in like little wings and opened his mouth for a snack. Lily did the same. My mom says they're cute with whipped cream on top. Today they were cute with shampoo bubbles on top.

"Okay ducky dudes, here's your bread—*quack*." I dropped pretend bread in each of their mouths, and they both chewed happily.

When you are little and you have turned yourself into a duck, all you really need is make-believe food to be happy. Those were the days.

I patted the ducks on their heads. "When you're old like me, life is complicated," I told them. "I need to write a song quick—*quack*! For real—*quack*. It has to be good, so everybody will want to sing it instead of Scarlett's song."

Leo started singing and splashing water. *"Quacking in the rain!"*

Lily laughed and splashed, too.

Just then . . . *bam!* An idea popped into my head. "When it stops raining, a rainbow comes out," I said. "That would be a good idea for a song."

The ducks stopped splashing and looked at me.

"People love rainbows," I said. "A song about a rainbow would be catchy."

"Quack!" Leo said.

"The first verse will be about the rain, and then the chorus will be about the sun coming out and the rainbow shining in the sky. Hop out, little duckies. I'm going to turn the shower on so it sounds like rain. That will help me write."

Leo hopped out and I wrapped him in a towel.

Lily held her arms out to me. She was too little to hop out by herself. I picked her up and wrapped her in a towel.

I turned on the shower.

The two ducks and I sat on the floor and listened. It sounded exactly like rain.

"Everything okay in there?" my dad called out from the kitchen.

"Yep!" I called back.

I started to sing. *"Oh, listen to the pitter-patter of the rain. . . ."*

"Pitter-patter—quack!" Leo said.

"This is not silly," I said. "I'm writing a serious song about a rainbow. I want it to be sad at first like the rain."

Leo hopped up and waddled around like a silly duck ballerina and made rain fall on Lily's head with his fingers.

Lily giggled.

I chased them both out of the bathroom.

"Pitter-patter—quack," Leo sang, and they raced up the stairs. I chased after them. When I got to the top of the stairs, they were gone and it was quiet. I tiptoed into their room. And then they jumped out from behind the door and quacked. With their little ducky fingers, they tickled me in the place where I'm the most ticklish—the backs of my knees.

And then we heard a sound . . . a sound more terrible than a tornado . . . more horrible than a hurricane . . . more earth-shattering than an earthquake. . . . It was the sound of my dad's angry voice.

"Lucy McGee!"

Normally I like my name. But at that moment I wanted a different one.

"Lucy McGee!" he called again, and I ran down.

My dad was standing in the bathroom, which was flooded with soapy water.

"How could you have forgotten to turn off the shower?" he yelled.

Just then my mom walked in the door. "Uh-oh," she said. "What's going on?"

I tucked my arms in like little wings and said, "Me go—*quack*?"

Chapter Four

NOT MERRY OR VERY MERRY?

After I cleaned up the bathroom, I did all my homework. In my closet.

When I am upset, I sit on my special pillow in my closet. It isn't a big closet, but it has a light. When I am sitting in there, I like the way my clothes hang down around my head. It's like I'm alone in the jungle, and there are vines all around me.

I don't like to talk. But sometimes I write notes to my parents and slip them under the closet door into my bedroom.

Leo knows this. He comes into my bedroom and checks for notes. If there is a note on the floor, he pretends he is an owl and hoots very softly so I know he's there. And then he picks up the note in his owl beak and flies away to deliver it.

After I was in my closet a while, I wrote a note.

Dear Dad and Mom,

I'm very sorry.

In case you're wondering, I did all my homework. And I'm still not coming out of this closet. If you hear sounds, it's probably me crying. I am not having a good day because I need to write a song for the big talent show.

I was trying to write it, and then Leo and Lily did the tickle thing and I forgot about the shower. The problem is Leo and Lily are cute. This should make you feel good. When I grow up I hope my kids are cute. But I don't want my kids to be too cute because then I'll forget things like turning off the shower and my house will have a flood. I hope I did a good job cleaning up. I tried hard.

By the way, Mrs. Brock wrote you a letter, too. It is in my backpack in the kitchen. You can save that one for another day, if you want. Too much reading is probably not good for your eyes. Too much crying isn't, either, but I can't stop.

My face is wet like the world outside. It has been a very watery day.

Your sad and sorry daughter,

Lucy

After Leo flew away, I waited and waited. I could smell pizza baking in the kitchen, and that made more tears come out of me because I was hungry and if I stayed in my closet forever, I would never taste pizza again.

Then there was a little running sound and a *"Hoot, hoot."*

A note came under the door.

Dear Lucy,

You did a good job cleaning up. And we are glad you did your homework. We read the letter from Mrs. Brock. We need to talk about how to help you with time. We love that you want to sing in the talent show, but you have to pay attention during school.

Come out and we'll talk.

It's almost time for dinner.

Love,

Your dad and mom

I opened the door and hugged Leo. Then we ran downstairs to the kitchen.

Mom, Dad, Leo, and Lily all squashed me in another hug.

"Do you understand that Mrs. Brock wants you to follow directions?" Mom asked.

I nodded.

"When it's time for math, that means do math," Dad said. "When it's time for science . . ."

"I'll do science!" I said.

"When it's time to tickle . . . ," Leo said. "Tickle—*quack*." He turned back into a duck and tickled me.

Lily turned into a duck again and tickled Mom. And then Mom and Dad both turned into ducks and started tickling all of us.

"Be a duck too—*quack*," Leo said to me.

"The more the merrier—*quack*," my dad said.

I flapped my wings. The more the quackier! A very merry flock!

Chapter Five

MY SING-ALONG SONG

After dinner, I wrote a song!

THE TOGETHER SONG

BY LUCY MCGEE

One duck floating in a pond is nice to see.
But a flock floating together is sweeter than sweet.

The more we float together,
the more we float together,
the more the merrier we'll be.

A lion roaming all alone might want to cry.
But if her friends all join her, she's got her pride.

The more we roam together,
the more we roam together,
the more the merrier we'll be.

A dolphin swimming solo is so odd.
They have way more fun
swimming in a pod.

The more we swim together,
the more we swim together,
the more the merrier we'll be.

Fish love a school.
Horses love a team.
Wolves love a pack.
That's what they need.

Somehow you + you + me
equals more than three.
'Cause when we sing together,
we sing joyfully.

The more we sing together,
the more we sing together,
the more the merrier we'll be.

Chapter Six

SPIES AND LIES!

When I woke up, my tooth was so loose, I could push it out with my tongue like a little door. When you've got a loose tooth in your mouth and a new song in your backpack, life is good. The sun was having a good day, too. No big bully clouds bringing rain.

Everybody was outside, lining up to wait for the bell to start school. Most of the kids in my class like to stand on the blacktop by the school doors. Phillip and I sometimes meet by the fence. Today he was waiting there for me.

"You look happy," Phillip said.

"I am," I said. "I wrote a great new song!"

Just then, Scarlett was walking past us toward the blacktop. She stopped and looked over at us.

"Just wave and smile like there's nothing going on," Phillip said. We both waved and smiled. She gave us a funny look and walked over to Victoria and Mara.

"I wrote a song during dinner last night, but it's too short," Phillip said.

He sang:

Pass the mashed potatoes,
so hot and butter scented.
But not the mushed-up peas, please.
I wish they weren't invented.

"As you might have guessed," he said, "I don't like peas."

I laughed.

Scarlett looked over at us again.

"Sing me your song," he said.

I sang it softly so Scarlett couldn't hear it.

"Wow," Phillip said. "I like the words a lot!"

The look he got on his face made me feel good. He really liked it!

He had some great ideas for more words. Together we

made the song longer. Scarlett kept giving us suspicious looks.

"Let's go over and sing our song to everybody," I said.

Phillip stopped me. "Wait! I think it will be better if we spy on them at recess. We'll listen to Scarlett sing her song and then we'll jump out and sing ours."

It was a dramatic idea. I loved it!

The bell rang and we ran in.

During class I wanted to sing the song over and over in my head, but I didn't. When it was time for spelling, I spelled. When it was time for math, I mathed. When it was time for science, I scienced. When it was time for lunch, I ate like a pig. I had a sandwich with crunchy peanut butter, tortilla chips, and an apple. I crunched and munched a whole bunch, and my tooth still didn't come out!

Finally, it was time for recess. I couldn't find the paper with the song's words on it, but it didn't matter. I had the whole song memorized.

We waited until Scarlett gathered her little group by the picnic table, and then we crept over and hid behind the tree near the table. Nobody saw us.

"Okay, I just wrote this song for us today," Scarlett was saying. "And—"

"Wait," Resa said. "Why aren't Lucy and Phillip here? They're fourth graders, and they're part of the Songwriting Club."

"I asked Lucy and Phillip," Scarlett said. "But they said they wanted to do their own thing."

Behind the tree Phillip and I looked at each other. Our eyes were popping out of our heads. What a liar!

"Let's hear your song," Pablo said.

Scarlett took a piece of paper out of her pocket and started singing.

One duck floating in a pond is
nice to see.
But a flock floating together
is sweeter than sweet.

The more we float together,
the more we float together,
the more the merrier we'll be.

What? I jumped out and yelled, "Hey, I wrote that song!"

Chapter Seven

FIGHT FOR WHAT'S RIGHT

"Lucy is right," Phillip said. "Scarlett did not write that song!"

Scarlett made a surprised face. "What are you guys talking about?"

"You stole my words, Scarlett!" I said.

Scarlett rolled her eyes and held out her paper.

"This is my handwriting. It says right here. 'The Together Song' by Scarlett Tandy."

I grabbed it and looked at it. "You wrote down my words and put your name on the paper. You just made up a different tune. That's not fair!"

"Prove it," Scarlett said.

"Lucy is telling the truth," Phillip said. "She showed me her song this morning, and we added new stuff to it."

"You two should get married," Scarlett said. "You're always sticking up for each other."

Victoria and Mara laughed.

My face got hot. I crumpled up the paper and threw it at her.

"Hold on," Pablo said, picking up the paper. "It sounds like a perfect song for the show."

The others gathered around to read the words.

"I like it a lot," Resa said. She looked at me and Phillip. "Great job on the words."

Resa believed us!

Saki and Natalie nodded. They believed us, too.

"Great job on the tune," Victoria said, looking at Scarlett.

"Yeah," Mara added. "Really great tune."

Scarlett's tune was better than mine, but I didn't want to admit it.

"I think we should all do the song together," Resa said. "The whole Songwriting Club."

Pablo, Natalie, and Saki agreed right away.

"I guess I can live with that," Scarlett said.

I was still mad because Scarlett lied and didn't admit it, but I didn't want to miss the show.

I looked at Phillip to see what he thought. Phillip has a good brain.

"Here's what we do. We use our words and Scarlett's tune. And we all sing." Phillip gave Scarlett a look. "The more the merrier."

Scarlett shrugged. "If I had known you guys wanted to sing with us, I would have invited you."

I started getting mad again. But then Saki started singing the song and everybody joined in, and that made me feel better.

We practiced the song a bunch of times. Every time I looked at Scarlett, I got mad all over again. So, I looked at Phillip's nose instead.

"We sound amazing," Pablo said.

We did!

I was in a good mood all afternoon. And then we had a surprise at the end of the day.

It was our hamster's birthday. Mrs. Brock brought out a little hamster cake for Mr. Chomper made of oat cereal, sesame seeds, and honey, and we sang "Happy Birthday." She also had delicious cupcakes with chocolate frosting and sprinkles for us.

"Yum!" I said. "Maybe when I eat this, my tooth will finally fall out." As I was about to take a cupcake, Scarlett gave me a look.

"You still have baby teeth?" she asked. "I lost all mine ages ago."

"Me too," Mara said.

I shrugged.

Scarlett gave me another look. "You know, if your tooth falls out, you'll have a hole in your smile, and that will make you look babyish in the talent show."

Everybody looked at me.

"Famous singers always have very nice teeth," Scarlett said. "Don't let it come out until after the show, Lucy. If one person looks bad, we'll all look bad."

"Scarlett, that's not true," Mrs. Brock said. "And Lucy can't help it if her tooth falls out."

"It's not going to fall out!" I said quickly, and put the cupcake back. "It's hardly even loose."

"It'll be fine either way, Lucy," Mrs. Brock said. "Go ahead and eat one."

I stared at the cupcakes. Then I thought

about how I would look with a big old hole in the middle of my smile.

"I'm not hungry," I said.

Scarlett smiled with all her adult teeth and ate the biggest one.

Chapter Eight

MY FEARS AND LEO'S TEARS

When you do not eat the special snack at school that everyone else eats, it's hard to be cheerful. By the time I got home I was grumpy. I walked in the door and what did I smell? Crunchzels!

"Oh no!" I cried. Crunchzels are treats my dad makes with chocolate, peanut butter, and crunchy pretzels.

My dad was wiping chocolate off Lily's face. He looked up and asked, "Now what?"

"You made Crunchzels!" I yelled.

"What's wrong with that? You love Crunchzels!" he said. "I made them to try and cheer up Leo."

Lily reached for another one.

I did the only thing I could do. I went up to my closet and opened the door. And then I screamed because a wolf was in my closet.

It wasn't a real wolf. It was Leo acting like a wolf. Well, more like a wolf puppy.

"*Aawooo!*" he howled.

"What are you doing in here?"

He peeked out so I could see his whole head. His hair was way shorter. His eyes were red, and his face was wet from crying.

"You got a haircut," I said. "And you hate it?"

He nodded.

"Your hair looks cute," I said.

"I look like a baby," he said. "I'm too sad to eat." Then he howled again. "*Aawooo!*"

"I know how you feel, Leo," I said. "I'm sad, too. And I can't ever eat again. If I lose my tooth, I'll look bad in the show."

He lifted up his sad face. Then he stood and gave me a hug.

Getting a hug from a sad, hungry wolf puppy has a funny way of cheering a person up.

"I have an idea for you," I said.

I looked in my closet until I found my old brown winter hat. Then I found some brown paper and cut out two triangles. I put the shapes on the hat with safety pins in just the right places and put the hat on Leo's head. Then I took him over to the mirror.

"Look," I said. "It's a wolf-puppy hat. It will totally hide your hair."

Leo smiled. He put up his paws and yipped, and then he licked my cheek.

"Okay, wolf puppy," I said. "Run and play. I am going to practice my song in the mirror. Our Songwriting Club is meeting tomorrow after school, and I want to be perfect."

The wolf puppy ran downstairs. He probably ate three Crunchzels.

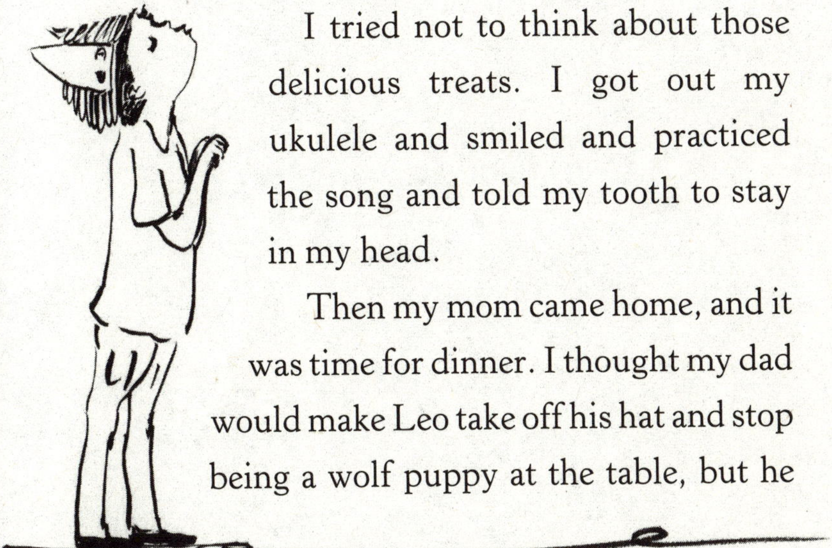

I tried not to think about those delicious treats. I got out my ukulele and smiled and practiced the song and told my tooth to stay in my head.

Then my mom came home, and it was time for dinner. I thought my dad would make Leo take off his hat and stop being a wolf puppy at the table, but he didn't. I think my dad was having one of those days where a happy wolf puppy is way better than a howling kid.

It was a good night for everyone but me. I was too afraid to eat! I drank milk and had two bites of mashed potatoes. My stomach growled as loudly as a pack of wolves all night. *Aawooo!*

Chapter Nine

MY SLICK TRICK

When I got to school, I was grumpy because I wouldn't eat breakfast.

Phillip and I were at the end of the line walking into the school building. The others were all ahead of us, including Resa. And then something amazing happened. Resa slowed down until she was standing right next to us.

"Can I talk to you guys about Scarlett?" she asked.

By that time Scarlett was already inside the school doors.

We nodded.

Resa started doing what my dad calls "venting." We have a vent in our kitchen above our stove. When there's something burning on the stove, he pushes a button and a fan inside the vent takes the smoke and heat and yucky smell and sends it through the vent to the outside of our house! He says that sometimes people burn with big emotions and they need to let their feelings out. He calls that venting. Resa was full of emotion, and she needed to vent it out.

"I don't know what to do," she said to us. "Sometimes Scarlett is really nice to me and wants me to be her friend. But sometimes she is mean to other people, and that bothers me. I love her tune, but it wasn't right for her to steal your words. Anyway, she just gave me a note saying you guys should stand in the back when we sing. That's not right, either. I don't know what to do."

"A note?" Phillip frowned. "Can we see it?"

Resa looked worried. "It's mean. Are you sure you want to see it?"

My face started getting hot.

"Yes!" Phillip said.

I wasn't so sure.

"Scarlett told me to pass the note to Victoria and Mara, but I didn't," Resa said. "Don't tell her I gave it to you."

"We won't," Phillip said.

"Promise?" she asked.

"Promise," we both said.

She handed Phillip the note. He read it out loud.

Hi Resa,

My mom is buying amazing costumes for all of us for the talent show! They will be the best!

When we sing the song for the show, I think you and me and Victoria and Mara should be in the front. You all have really pretty hair and pretty voices, and you'll look so good in the costumes. Wear your fanciest shoes! Lucy and Phillip should stand way in the back. Even if Lucy's tooth doesn't fall out, her hair is too flat, and Phillip is too short. I don't want to hurt their feelings. I just know the whole group will look really good with us in the front. Let's practice at recess! Pass this on to Victoria and Mara.

See ya,

Scarlett

I felt burning hot now.

"Scarlett doesn't know anything!" Phillip said. "Your hair is nice, and I am not too short."

I nodded, but I could tell Scarlett had hurt his feelings, too.

As we walked into the school, I crumpled up Scarlett's note. "At least nobody else is going to read this," I said. "Thanks for not passing it on, Resa."

A sad sound came out of Phillip like the air coming out of a bouncy ball. "She can always write a new one," he said.

It was true.

"What are you guys going to do?" Resa asked. "Do you want to be in the show with her? What should I do?"

We turned down the hallway toward our classroom, and an idea popped into my head.

Phillip stopped. "Lucy, you have a funny look on your face."

"I have an idea for a trick I can play on Scarlett. It might teach her a lesson," I said.

"Tell us!" Phillip said.

By that time we were already in our room, and Mrs. Brock wanted us to get ready for the morning.

"You'll see!" I whispered to both of them.

While everybody was putting their stuff away in their cubbies, I got a piece of paper. Very carefully, I wrote a new note, copying Scarlett's handwriting.

Hi Victoria!

This is Scarlett. When we sing our song, I think I should be in the front because my hair is way prettier than anybody else's hair. I'm waaaaay prettier than you and Mara and Resa. Let's practice at recess!

See ya,

Scarlett

I snuck behind Victoria and slipped the note into her math notebook. Resa and Phillip saw me. I could tell they were dying to know what the note said!

When I am doing something sneaky, I get this buzzy feeling inside. Right then, I felt like a swarm of bees were buzzing inside of me.

During math I saw Victoria open her notebook and find the note. Her face turned red.

While Mrs. Brock wasn't looking, Victoria passed the note to Mara. I watched Mara's face get even madder. My trick was working!

Then Mara showed the note to Resa and passed it back to Victoria. When no one was looking, Resa gave me a look. "Did you write it?" she whispered.

I nodded and grinned. I wasn't sure what was going to happen, but I had a feeling it was going to be good.

Chapter Ten

ART ROOM DOOM!

Right after Victoria, Mara, and Resa read the mean note that I wrote in Scarlett's handwriting, it was time for art. Victoria, Mara, and Scarlett always walk to art together. Except today. Today, Victoria grabbed Mara and Resa. The three of them walked out of the room together. Quickly.

"Wait!" Scarlett said. She ran to catch up with them. She had on her fancy shoes with the little heels that went *click, click, click.* Victoria and Mara wouldn't look at her. They were too mad. Resa looked back at me.

"What's going on?" Phillip whispered. "Why is Resa looking at you? Why are Victoria and Mara mad at Scarlett?"

I didn't have time to explain because Mr. Hopkin was waiting for us at the door. I gave Phillip my wait-and-see look.

"We're going to be painting posters for the Fall Talent Show today," Mr. Hopkin said. "Make sure they're colorful. We'll hang them all over the school when they're dry."

There were cups of paint and big pieces of paper set out on the tables. Mr. Hopkin lets us sit wherever we want as long as we don't talk loudly.

"This is going to be fun," Scarlett said to the girls. "Let's sit together."

"I don't think so," Victoria said, and pulled Mara and Resa over to a table with three empty stools.

Scarlett stood there, shocked.

Mwa-ha-ha! Finally, Scarlett was getting the chance to see how it feels to be left out.

"Scarlett, find a seat!" Mr. Hopkin said.

Scarlett huffed and went over to a different table.

Phillip and I sat at Jeremy Bing's table.

"Lucy, what's going on?" Phillip whispered.

"I wrote a mean note to Victoria from Scarlett," I whispered back. "Now they're mad at Scarlett."

Scarlett was pretending not to be upset.

She was decorating her poster with pink polka dots.

Victoria was too mad to paint. She grabbed a piece of scrap paper, scribbled something on it, and passed it to Scarlett when Mr. Hopkin wasn't looking.

It must have been something bad, because Scarlett crumpled it up. A look came over her face. She poured black and red and purple paint into a cup and mixed them together. Then she walked over and dumped the paint on Victoria's hair!

Victoria screamed.

"Oh, I'm so sorry!" Scarlett said. "I tripped."

"You did that on

purpose, Scarlett!" Victoria cried. Then she threw her paint on Scarlett's hair!

It was crazy. Scarlett and Victoria both stood there, dripping with paint. I didn't think my note would lead to this!

"Girls!" Mr. Hopkin yelled. "What's going on?"

Scarlett started crying. "It's about our song for the talent show. Victoria wrote a mean note." She held up the crumpled paper. "It said that I am too tall. And I can't be in the front. Ever."

Victoria started crying. "I wrote that because Scarlett wrote a mean note to me saying her hair is prettier."

"I did not," Scarlett said.

Victoria pulled my note out of her back pocket and gave it to her.

Scarlett stopped crying. "I didn't write this.

Somebody copied my handwriting."

Mr. Hopkin looked at all of us. "Does anyone in this room know anything about this?"

Resa and Phillip looked at me.

Oh no! The right thing to do was to tell the truth, but now I was really scared.

The big black clock on the wall went *tick, tick, tick*. The paint from Scarlett's and Victoria's hair went *drip, drip, drip*.

Should I confess or shouldn't I? Should I or shouldn't I?

Before I could decide, Jeremy Bing raised his hand. "Um . . . I think I heard Lucy whispering about that."

Everybody looked at me.

Scarlett's face burned. "You wrote this note, Lucy McGee!"

Chapter Eleven

TRY NOT TO CRY

At the time, writing a fake note in Scarlett's handwriting seemed like a perfect way to teach her a lesson. Now it seemed like a perfect way to get in trouble.

Scarlett turned to Victoria and Mara and Resa. "You guys are my best friends," she said. "I would never write a note like that."

Victoria looked embarrassed. "I'm sorry I poured paint on you, Scarlett! I was so mad."

"People who write mean notes shouldn't be allowed to do extra things at school, like be in the Fall Talent Show," Mara said, and gave me a mean look.

"But I wrote that note because Scarlett wrote a much meaner note about me and Phillip and gave it to Resa," I said. Then I gulped. I had promised Resa I wouldn't tell.

Scarlett gave Resa a mean look.

"Sorry, Resa," Phillip said. "I know we promised, but this is an emergency!" He pulled Scarlett's first note out of his pocket. "See, it's true. I have the proof right here." He gave it to Mr. Hopkin.

Scarlett said quickly, "It was just a joke. Really. You guys need to learn to take a joke." Then she turned to Mr. Hopkin and said in her sweetest voice, "I'm sorry about the mess, Mr. Hopkin. Victoria and I will clean up the paint."

"Scarlett, you and Victoria need to go to the bathroom and wash the paint out of your hair. Lucy, you can clean up the floor in here. Writing notes and throwing paint are not good ways to solve problems," he said. "Look at this room. The three of you should come back after school and do more cleaning. I'll e-mail your parents to let them know."

"But after school today we have a Songwriting Club meeting," Phillip said.

"Victoria, Scarlett, and Lucy will have to miss it," Mr. Hopkin said. "Everybody back to work."

What a nightmare!

After school I had to go to the art room with Scarlett and Victoria.

While we mopped the floor and wiped the tables, the girls whispered to each other. I had a lot of sad and mad feelings inside me that wanted to come out by crying. But if I cried, Scarlett would call me a baby. So I vented all those feelings out by wiping the tables really, really hard. I'm sorry, tables!

On the way out, Scarlett said, "Victoria, Mara, and I are going to sing a song together for the show. It won't be a Songwriting Club thing. It will just be our thing."

Victoria nodded. "Just our thing. We don't want Resa, either, because she gave you Scarlett's note."

"Fine," I said. "I wouldn't want to sing with you if you gave me a million dollars."

"Fine," Scarlett said. "We're not asking you."

"Fine," I said. "But you can't sing 'The Together Song' because I wrote the words."

"Fine," she said. "But you can't sing it, either, because I wrote the tune."

"Fine," I said. "I'll write a new one."

It wasn't fine, though. I really liked that song!

They walked off.

By the time I got to the fence, Phillip was there with his ukulele.

"How was cleaning?" he asked.

"Terrible," I said. "How was Songwriting Club?"

"Sad," he said. "It isn't the same without you. Ms. Adamson thinks we should all skip the talent show since it's causing so many problems."

"Scarlett is going to do a song with just Victoria and Mara," I said.

He made a face. "Maybe we should do one with just you and me and Resa," he said.

"Resa won't want to sing with us. We broke our promise."

"Well, we could do it with just you and me," he said.

"We'd have to write another song," I said sadly. "I don't know if I have it in me."

"Come on, Lucy," Phillip said. "We can't let Scarlett win."

He made a fist and held it up in the air like the hero in a movie. "We can do this!" he said. "We can do this!"

Phillip's good energy spilled into me.

"You're right, Phillip!" I said. "Let's rock that show!"

Chapter Twelve

HAIR WITH FLAIR

On the way home, my good energy faded away. I thought about how sad it was not to be singing "The Together Song" with everybody. I thought about how mad Resa must be at me and Phillip. That made me sad. I liked Resa. I also thought about how Scarlett and her group were going to look

amazing in their store-bought costumes. And I thought about how Phillip and I wouldn't seem good compared to them.

But my brain didn't stop there. I also thought about how my hair would look. I always thought I had good hair. But maybe Scarlett was right. Maybe it was too flat. Maybe it needed to be . . . more puffy. I thought about things that are puffy. Cupcakes. Donuts. Pillows. I thought about things that are flat. Bad cupcakes. Bad donuts. Bad pillows. Oh no! I had bad hair. If I was going to sing in the talent show, I needed better hair.

But my brain kept going down, down, down. I also thought about how my dad was going to act when I got home. Mr. Hopkin must have e-mailed him about the fake note I wrote and how it led to a paint fight. I hoped my dad was having a fun day, because then he wouldn't be as mad.

I walked in the door. Lily was sitting on the kitchen floor crying. My dad was sweeping with a broom. Our big plant in the blue pot was tipped over. The pot was broken and there was dirt all over the floor.

Lily looked at me and cried harder. "Me boke it."

Then the sound of howling came from upstairs. Possibly in the direction of my closet. Leo was howling.

My dad gave me a look. It was not the look of a dad having a fun day.

Even though I was very upset about my own problems, an idea popped into my head. If you make a mistake, say you're sorry and do a good deed as soon as you can. If it was a big mistake, do a whole bunch of good deeds. When your parents look at you, they'll just remember your good deeds because they're old, and they can't remember a whole lot, which is why they're always forgetting where they put the car keys.

"I know Mr. Hopkin e-mailed about the mean note I wrote. I'm sorry," I said quickly. "I was going to go up to my closet and have a howl, but I can hear that Leo is doing that. So I'll take Lily up there and give you a little peace and quiet, Dad. That's a good deed because you can have a nap. You look like you need one."

He gave me a surprised look.

I did another good deed by picking up Lily, which made her stop crying. But snot was coming out of her nose, which was gross, so I set her down.

"I don't exactly have time for a nap, but thank you, Lucy," my dad said. "I would appreciate some peace and quiet while I clean up. We'll talk about what happened today when Mom comes home. This talent show seems to be causing a lot of problems."

"Since I said sorry and since I got Lily to stop crying and since I'm going to get Leo to stop howling, that will be three good deeds I'm doing," I said.

"Yes, it will," he said.

I grabbed a tissue and wiped Lily's gross nose. "I'm doing another good deed! Four new good deeds is way better than one bad deed. That should make you happy, right?"

My dad smiled a tiny bit. But then he said, "We'll talk about it later, Lucy."

Lily held my hand, and we walked upstairs to my room. We both looked at the closet door. And then Lily crawled onto my bed and sat there, sucking her thumb.

"*Aawooo.*" Leo's little voice sounded sadder than ever.

"Leo, stop howling," I said.

"*Aawooo,*" Leo howled again.

"Leo, tell me what's wrong," I said. "Maybe I can fix it."

I heard a rustling sound, and then the door opened a little. "I had to sit in the time-out chair at school," he said.

Leo is in kindergarten. I tried to remember what kind of trouble you can get into when you're in kindergarten.

"What did you do?" I asked.

"Nothing."

"Leo." I opened the door some more. "Why did you have to sit in time-out?"

He had his hands over his hair. "Because I wouldn't take my wolf-puppy hat off," he sniffled. "My teacher told me it was getting in the way of learning. She took it."

"Leo, you have to be a kid during school," I said.

"A wolf puppy is better," he said.

"When teachers look out, they want to see twenty kids. They don't want to see nineteen kids and one wolf puppy," I said. "It throws them off."

He leaned his head back and howled.

An idea popped into my brain. I ran into the bathroom and got my mom's styling gel.

"Leo, cool dudes wear

styling gel," I said, and held up the tube. "I'm going to make you look like the coolest dude ever."

"Me coo, too!" Lily cried.

"Okay, I'll do you too, Lily." I patted the bed. "Hop up, Leo. Welcome to my hair salon!"

Leo stopped being sad and climbed up next to Lily.

Every great business has a great jingle, so I sang.

Is your hair a nightmare?
I care about hair! I repair hair! Oooh!
I dare to take the scare
right out of your hair! Oooh!
I'll turn it into hair with flair!
With your brand-new hair, I declare,
you'll feel like a millionaire!

They both clapped.

More rhymes from me, Lucy McGee. I'm good with rhymes. What can I say?

I gooped up one clump of Leo's hair and made a little spike. Not bad! I gooped all his hair and made little spikes all over his head. "I'm calling this hairstyle the Prickly Porcupine," I said. "It's very cool."

Lily clapped. "Me too! Me too!"

I gooped up Lily's hair. I made one braid that stuck out on the left side and another braid that stuck out on the right side. Finally, I made a pigtail on the very top and spiked all the ends. "I call this hairstyle the Piggy Longstocking," I said.

They looked in the mirror and both started dancing around.

"Hey, this gives me an idea," I said. "I'm

going to do myself. With a new hairstyle, my hair won't look so flat."

Sploosh went the goop. With the bottom half of my hair, I made ten little braids. With the top half, I made three stegosaurus spikes and two baby pigtails that stuck out like bug antennae. Once I got started, it was hard to stop.

We heard the door downstairs open, and my mom called up, "I'm home!"

Leo's smile dropped. "Mom won't like me for sitting in time-out."

I looked at Leo. "Even when they're mad, Mom and Dad love you. I got in trouble today, too. They're going to want to talk to both of us. When you're in trouble, parents want to talk and talk and talk. It's what they do. Just listen and nod."

He nodded.

"And then offer to do a good deed," I said. "That helps. A lot."

My mom and dad came up, and they almost screamed when they saw us. They were so surprised about our hair.

"Wow," my mom said. "You've been busy."

"We're both really sorry about today," I

said. "If you want, I can do your hair for free. Both of you! I can do all kinds of hairstyles, as you can see."

Leo and Lily smiled.

"That's okay," Mom said.

"If I don't make it as a famous songwriter," I said, "I can open Lucy's Hair Salon. It's fun to style hair."

"That is quite a backup plan," my dad said. "But no thank you on the hairstyle for me, either. I think it's time to clean up and have dinner."

"You guys should have had more kids," I said.

My dad groaned. "Why?"

"I want to do more hairstyling!" I said.

Chapter Thirteen

TUMMY DRAMA AND HEAD TRAUMA

My hair and I went to school in a good mood. My tooth was still in my head, too. It was going to be a great day.

Phillip was waiting for me by the fence. He looked sick. He had one hand on his stomach. His other hand was holding a big carton of milk.

"Your hair exploded," he said.

"It's my new style," I said. "It's not flat anymore."

"Did you do that because of what Scarlett wrote?" he asked.

"No," I said. "Are you sick? Why are you holding your stomach?"

"I'm fine," he said. "I'm just really, really, really full." He took another sip of milk.

"If you're so full, why are you drinking more?" I asked.

"No reason," he said, which made me think there was a reason.

As we walked to the school doors, he drank even more.

"Let's ask Resa if she wants to sing with us," I said. "Maybe if she says yes, then Saki and Natalie and Pablo will all say yes."

Scarlett, Victoria, and Mara were standing by the doors.

Scarlett saw me and started laughing. And then Victoria and Mara did, too. They were laughing at my hair.

The sound of laughter is a happy thing, my dad says. Well, it's not a happy sound when mean girls are laughing at your hair.

I did the only thing I could think of doing. I turned around and started to walk home.

The bell rang.

Phillip chased after me. "Lucy, what are you doing?"

"I'm feeling sick," I said. "I'm going home."

"I'm feeling sick, too," Phillip said. "I think I'll go home."

He took another sip.

"Phillip, why are you drinking when you feel sick?"

He got a funny look on his face. "I'm trying to grow faster."

What Scarlett had said about being short had gotten to him! Poor Phillip. I knew how he felt.

We made it to where the sidewalk started when Mr. Hopkin saw us. He had morning bus duty.

"Wrong direction," he said.

"I need to go home," Phillip said. "I have a problem with my stomach."

"I need to go home, too," I said. "I have a problem with my head."

He turned us both around and pointed us toward the school doors. "Get to class. No dawdling. No stopping. You're already late."

What would Mr. Hopkin know about bad hair? He doesn't even have any!

As we walked back into the building, Phillip started burping. Quickly, I pulled the hair bands off and undid all the braids. It felt different.

"Is my hair puffy?" I asked Phillip.

"Very." He nodded and rubbed his stomach. He looked even more sick.

"I think sleeping with my hair braided made it wavy," I said. "Does it look good?"

He shrugged. "I liked it fine the old way."

It was the nicest thing anybody ever said to me. He was about to take the last sip of milk, but I stopped him. "Phillip Lee, you are not too short."

He gave me a weak smile and tossed the carton into a recycling bin.

By the time we walked in, everybody had put away their backpacks and were sitting at their desks. They all looked at us.

And then Scarlett started laughing. Again.

I went over to the mirror by Mr. Chomper's cage and looked. The bottom half of my hair was crazy wavy. The top half of my hair was sticking up. Even Mr. Chomper the hamster was laughing.

There was a spray bottle of water on the counter. I picked it up and started spraying it all over my hair.

"No!" Mrs. Brock yelled. "That's not water! That's vinegar for cleaning Mr. Chomper's cage."

Vinegar was dripping down my head. I smelled like a salad!

"Yuck!" Mara said, and plugged her nose.

"Oh no!" Phillip said.

Everybody looked at him, and then he ran over to the trash can and threw up.

A lot.

The whole class started running and screaming. Even Resa.

Resa would never want to sing with us again. Nobody would.

"Class!" Mrs. Brock yelled. She made everybody sit down.

Phillip got to go home. I had to wash my hair in the sink and go back to class.

Not a fun day. At all.

Chapter Fourteen

TOOTH TRUTH

By the time I got home, my hair was flat and my stomach was growling. I didn't want my tooth to fall out, so I didn't eat lunch. You know how people say "I was so hungry I could have eaten a horse?" Well, I could have eaten a team of horses.

When I walked in the door, I heard my dad and

Leo and Lily playing upstairs.

At least somebody was having a good day.

One Crunchzel was left. It was sitting there, smelling like chocolatey goodness. I grabbed that baby and shoved it in my mouth.

Yum! Yum! Crunch!

I bit something hard. "Oh no!" I yelled.

I spit out my tooth! I ran to the mirror and looked at the hole in my mouth. I'd thought the day couldn't get any worse. It had gotten worse.

Leo and Lily came running down with my dad following.

"My tooth!" I screamed, and held it up.

"Yay!" Leo said. "You can get money from the tooth fairy!"

"I don't want money. I want my tooth back in my mouth!" I said. I marched over to the kitchen and threw that tooth into the trash can. Then I ran upstairs and sat in my closet.

Everybody wanted to cheer me up, but it couldn't be done.

"Come down, Lucy," my dad called up. "We're going to play in the backyard before dinner. Fresh air will be good for you."

"Fresh air will just blow through the big hole in my mouth and make it worse," I said.

While they played outside, I took my ukulele into my closet and wrote a new song.

I want to stay in my closet
right now.
I want to stay in my closet
and howl.

Everyone will hear me
and say, "Wow, oh wow.
We feel sorry for that kid
in the closet."

Aawooo! Aawooo!

I want to stay in my closet
and howl.
Don't try and make me
come out.

Don't cheer me up,
'cause I won't allow it.
Just feel sorry for the kid
in the closet.

Aawooo! Aawooo! Aawooo!

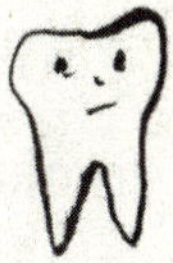

Singing and playing my ukulele always makes me feel better.

After a while a thought popped into my head. I should get that tooth out of the trash can and put it under my pillow. Money can't buy you happiness, but it's better than nothing. I tiptoed down to the kitchen.

The trash can was empty!

I ran to the back door and looked out. My dad must have taken the kitchen trash out to the big trash can. Now my tiny tooth was in that big can with all the gross stuff. I would never find it.

I went back upstairs and vented. I cried and howled very loudly, but nobody even heard me.

Finally, I was vented out. My mom came home, and we ate spaghetti and garlic bread. I told everybody how Scarlett was going to make fun of my smile, and they all told me not to listen to her. Easy for them to say.

"Well, it's good to see you are finally eating again," my mom said.

"What do you call a group of pigs?" I asked.

"A litter," my dad said.

"I was going to say I'm eating like a pig," I said. "But I'm really eating like a litter of pigs." I took another chomp of garlic bread.

"Tomorrow will be a better day," my mom said.

"I doubt it," I said. "But at least I'll be full."

I was tired, so I went to bed at the same time as Leo and Lily even though I am allowed to stay up half an hour later. When I put my head on my pillow, something sounded funny.

I lifted up my pillow. There was a note. I opened it up. It was written in my dad's handwriting. My tooth was at the bottom! It was taped onto the paper.

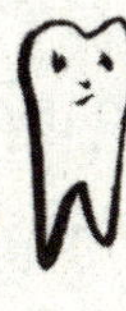

Dear Tooth Fairy,

This is Leo. I'm in kindergarten and my writing isn't good, so I'm telling my dad what to put here. This is Lucy's tooth! She did not mean to throw it out. Please give her extra money because this is a very nice tooth and because Lucy is very sad.

Love,

Leo

That made me so happy. I tiptoed into Leo and Lily's bedroom. They were both tucked in, and the light was already off.

"Leo," I whispered.

He opened his eyes.

"Thank you for getting my tooth," I said. "That was a really good deed."

"Are you done being sad?" he asked.

"I'm still a little sad, but you helped a lot."

I started tiptoeing out.

"Lucy!" he whispered.

"What?" I turned around.

"Tell me when you're all the way happy," he said.

I smiled. "Okay, Leo. Good night!"

Chapter Fifteen

FRIENDS AGAIN?

"I don't care if I'm short," Phillip said. He was waiting for me by the fence.

"I don't care if my hair is flat and my smile is holey," I said. I showed him the hole in my smile and the money I found under my pillow. "My dad is taking me to

Franklin's after school so I can buy candy. So that's one good thing."

"Yeah," he said. "And we're going to make a new song and be good in the talent show. We don't need anybody else." He held out his fist and I fist-bumped it.

"Okay, but I can't write a song during school, Phillip. My dad said if I got in trouble during school, he wouldn't take me for candy."

All day I was quiet and good.

After school my dad and Leo and Lily and I went downtown. We were about to walk into Franklin's Candy Store when a voice called out, "Lucy!"

We turned. Scarlett's babysitter ran up to us with Brandy, Scarlett's little sister. Catherine had been babysitting Brandy and Scarlett every day after school for years, so our family knew her.

"Hi, Catherine," my dad said. "How are you? Hi, Brandy. You're getting huge!"

They both said hi, and then Catherine said, "I'm worried about Scarlett."

"Scarlett's annoying," Brandy said, and rolled her eyes.

"That's what Lucy says," Leo blurted out.

My dad shushed him, and I turned red.

"Since Wednesday, Scarlett hasn't been eating," Catherine said. "She's also been walking around with a heavy book on her head. When I asked her why, she said she was trying to squash herself down because she's too tall. That's also why she's not eating. I dropped her off at gymnastics ten minutes ago, and they called to say she's feeling sick and needs to be picked up." Catherine turned to me. "Lucy, do you know if kids at school have been teasing Scarlett about being too tall?"

I didn't know what to say. I didn't write that note about Scarlett being too tall, but it was kind of my fault that Victoria wrote it.

"Lucy?" my dad asked. "Do you know anything about this?"

"I never said she's too tall," I said. "She doesn't seem sad at school."

"I think she's trying to hide how sad she is," Catherine said. "We all know Scarlett can be dramatic, but I think she's having a hard time right now. And I'm not sure how to help her. I can't change her height!"

My dad nodded. "I think this talent show is making all the kids worry too much. Right, Lucy?" He looked at me. "You've been worrying about your hair and your tooth falling out. That's been hard for you, too."

I turned even redder. The guys in my family sure talk a lot.

"Can you think of some way to help?" my dad asked.

Everybody was looking at me.

"I guess I could say something nice to Scarlett about how she isn't too tall," I said.

"That would be great, Lucy!" Catherine said. "Scarlett needs a boost."

We said goodbye. As we walked into Franklin's, my dad gave me a hug and said, "I'm proud of you for thinking of that, Lucy. I know it's hard to be nice to someone who hasn't been nice to you, but it's a sign of your big heart."

My heart didn't feel big. It felt small and crumpled.

While I picked out my candy, I thought about it. If I was nice to Scarlett, maybe she would be nice to me and we could all sing "The Together Song" for the show. Resa and all the others in our club would be so happy. Scarlett and Victoria and Mara are really good at singing. And there's the costumes. Scarlett's mom would get us costumes, and Scarlett's mom is rich.

I didn't want a small, sad heart. I wanted a huge, happy one, so I decided to go to Scarlett's and make things right.

When we got home, I went over to Scarlett's and knocked on the door. Catherine looked happy to see me. "Scarlett's in the backyard," Catherine said.

I walked around to the back, and Scarlett looked at me.

"What are you doing here?" she asked.

I held out a piece of candy.

She looked at it and then at me.

"It's not poison," I said. "I promise."

"Why are you giving it to me?" she asked.

"I'm trying to make up. I'm sorry about the note," I said. "Victoria didn't mean what she said in her note. She was just trying to get back at you. You're not too tall, Scarlett. We should all sing together."

Scarlett started to cry. Not fake tears, real tears. It made my throat feel funny.

"But it's true," she cried. "I'm too tall. And I don't play the ukulele or sing as good as you and Phillip."

I couldn't believe my ears.

She went on. "My problem is that I get a picture in my mind of how I want things to be. I got this picture in my mind of me being in the front row when we sing our song for the talent show, and it's a really nice picture." She looked at me and wiped her nose with the back of her hand.

"It's true, Lucy. I like being in the

front row of things!" Scarlett sobbed. "And then I got really worried that Ms. Adamson would put you and Phillip in the front because you guys play and sing better than me. And you're short and I'm too tall!"

I was shocked. Scarlett was saying she was jealous of me and Phillip!

"That's not all," she cried. "My mom said she wouldn't buy us costumes, either."

I could tell she was sadder than sad. It's hard when you think you're going to get something special, and then you find out it was just your imagination.

"Scarlett," I said. "We could sing the song together. We could be friends again."

"You aren't mad at me for what I wrote?"

I handed her the candy.

She smiled a real smile and took it. "Thanks, Lucy."

While she ate it, I thought about how amazing candy was. Whenever one country is mad at another country, they should give each other candy. If they did that, we wouldn't have any wars.

She started singing the song.

An idea popped into my head. "We could make our own costumes. We could put glitter on white T-shirts. We'd all look really good."

"I love glitter, Lucy!" Scarlett said. "That is the best idea ever." She started jumping up and down.

When someone jumps up and down, I do, too. That's the way I am. My mom says I am easily infected by feelings.

"Can you come over tomorrow?" she asked. "It will be so much fun. Bring a white T-shirt and all the glitter you have. We can make costumes for us and then show everybody else."

She started singing the song, and I joined in.

The more we sing together,
the more the merrier we'll be.

Life is a surprise. I couldn't wait to tell Phillip and Resa and everybody else.

I sang and danced all the way home. When I got there, I said to Leo, "Hey, my heart is all the way happy!"

He gave me such a huge hug, it knocked me over. And of course, Lily jumped on top of us!

Chapter Sixteen

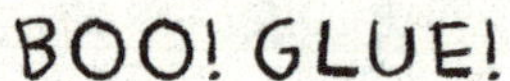

BOO! GLUE!

If you're me, it's hard to find a white T-shirt. I had three, but none of them were good. One had a rip from the time Leo was pretending to be a tiger. One had a grass stain from when Leo and Lily and I were pretending to be meatballs rolling out the door. And one was just plain dirty.

I took the grass-stained shirt and a jar of glitter over to Scarlett's after lunch on Sunday. I was going to go on Saturday, but Scarlett forgot she had gymnastics that day.

"Yay!" she said when I got to her house.

As everybody knows, Scarlett's house is fancy, so I took off my shoes. We went to her bedroom, which is also fancy. Her walls are pink, but her carpeting, bedspread, and pillows are all white. I went in and sat on her bed.

Yow! I sat on her cat, which was also white!

Princess Coconut screeched and jumped off the bed.

"Sorry, I didn't see you," I said to the cat.

The cat gave me a mean look. Princess Coconut does not like me.

"Look!" Scarlett said. "I made costume sketches! Which should we do?"

She set out a drawing with three different T-shirts. One had unicorns all over it. One had kittens. And one had unicorns and kittens.

"These look hard," I said. "And they don't really have to do with our song."

"They aren't hard," she said. "And they're really pretty."

Just then her mom walked in. "Hi girls. Why don't you come and work at the kitchen table? I'll get you some snacks."

I got up, but Scarlett kept looking at the sketches.

"We want to work in here," Scarlett said. "Brandy is annoying."

"I am okay working in the kitchen," I said.

Mrs. Tandy smiled at me, but then Scarlett snapped, "No way. I'm not moving."

My dad wouldn't let me talk that way, but Mrs. Tandy got a tray of snacks and brought them to us. Fruit punch in pretty glasses and little gooey brownies. *Yum!*

"Just be neat and work on your desk," her mom said. "Don't get anything on the carpet, okay?"

"Don't be such a worrier," Scarlett said.

Her mom left.

Scarlett got a big box of craft supplies. "This will be easier to do on the floor," she said.

"Your mom said we should work on your desk," I said.

She rolled her eyes. "We'll be careful and neat. Come on and help!"

She set the shirts on the floor and got out glue and glitter. "You paint on the glue, and then I'll put the glitter on." She handed me a

paintbrush and poured some glue onto a paper plate. Then she poured some glitter onto another paper plate.

Princess Coconut slinked toward us. I was worried the cat would step in the glue, so I picked up the plate.

Just then Brandy opened the door and yelled, "Boo!"

The cat jumped and knocked against my hand. Scarlett jumped, too. The glue and glitter went all over Princess Coconut.

The cat screeched and ran out of the room.

Brandy laughed.

Scarlett yelled at her and jumped up, knocking over the fruit punch.

Oh no! The white carpeting now had a big red puddle.

Scarlett chased after Brandy, yelling, "You brat!"

I jumped up to get a towel from the bathroom and stepped on a brownie.

Mrs. Tandy, Scarlett, and Brandy were all yelling in the hallway, and then they came in.

Scarlett was holding a gluey, glittery Princess Coconut.

Her mom looked at the mess on the floor. "What on earth happened?"

Scarlett yelled, "Brandy tried to scare us, and she made a huge mess."

Brandy pointed to me. "Lucy made the mess. I was just walking into the room. It's not my fault they got scared."

"She's lying!" Scarlett screamed, and made a face at Brandy.

"I hate you!" Brandy yelled, and made a face back.

"You're a brat," Scarlett said. "I hate you more." They started pushing each other, and the cat jumped out of Scarlett's arms and ran out of the room.

"Girls!" Mrs. Tandy yelled. "Stop it right now! Take that cat into the bathroom and clean her up. I'm going to have to pay to have this carpet cleaned." She grabbed our T-shirts and threw them in the trash.

"Now what are we going to wear for the

talent show?" Scarlett cried. "You wouldn't buy us real costumes! We were just trying to make our own! If Brandy hadn't—"

Her mom's eyebrows went up in a scary way. "You can forget about being in that talent show, Scarlett," she said.

Scarlett ran, crying, out of the room.

Brandy left, too.

I had a shivery feeling inside. It's strange being in a quiet room after people were yelling in it. I didn't know what to do, so I started trying to clean up the mess.

Mrs. Tandy turned and said, "Lucy, go home."

Of all the things she could say to me, that was the best.

Chapter Seventeen

HOME SWEET HOME

When I got home, my dad was making banana bread. He had flour on his nose and all over his T-shirt. He gave me a look. "Mrs. Tandy called," he said.

"It really wasn't my fault!" I said. "I wanted to work in the kitch—"

"Actually, Mrs. Tandy wasn't mad at you," he said.

"She wasn't?"

"She was upset with Scarlett and Brandy," he said. "She just wanted me to know that she was sending you home."

"I'm not in trouble?" I asked.

"No." He poured the batter into a pan. "What happened over there?"

"The Tandys all had a big fight," I said. "They were venting, but not in a good way. Sometimes when I'm over there, the way they talk to each other makes me get a shiver."

Just then Leo and Lily ran in. Leo hugged one of my legs and Lily hugged the other. They were like little koala bears hugging a tree, and I was the tree!

"Come and play," Leo said.

They made me feel the opposite of shivery. It was so good to be home. I wrote a song about it!

WHEN I'M HOME

BY LUCY MCGEE

When I feel sad and shivery,
home is where I want to be.
That's where I know I belong—
Me and my family.

Oh, when I'm home . . .
Oh, when I'm home . . .
So much can happen in an ordinary day.
I know that when I'm home, I'll be okay.

Though our clothes are kind of worn out,
torn right where they shouldn't be,
And our hair's a mess . . .
nothing fancy's fine with me.

Oh, when I'm home . . .
Oh, when I'm home . . .
So much can happen in an ordinary day.
I know that when I'm home, I'll be okay.

Inside jokes and made-up games
and noisy laugh-out-louds.
Sometimes we hug so hard
we knock each other down.

Home Sweet Home, Oh!
Home Sweet Home, Oh!
Home is where I want to go.
There I'll be okay.

Oh, when I'm home . . .
Oh, when I'm home . . .
So much can happen in an ordinary day.
I know that when I'm home, I'll be okay.

Chapter Eighteen

TOGETHER FOREVER

On Monday, Phillip was waiting for me by the fence.

I was about to tell him what happened at Scarlett's house, and then Resa walked up.

"Please don't say you're mad at us," Phillip said. "Because all this mad stuff is getting to me."

Resa smiled and shrugged. "I'm not mad. I just

came over to see if you heard about Scarlett."

I was about to tell them that I actually felt sorry for Scarlett when Scarlett came running over. She had a big smile on her face.

"I can be in the show!" she said. "I begged and begged, and my mom gave in. Let's practice at recess. We can have a dress rehearsal after school on Wednesday. I have a new idea for costumes. I can't believe the show is this Friday! It's going to be so much fun. Your words and my tune!" She hugged me and Phillip and then ran to tell Saki.

Resa grinned.

Phillip was shocked. "She hugged me," he said.

We laughed. Like I said, life is a surprise.

We all practiced at recess, and it was fun.

Scarlett's idea for costumes was great: jeans on the bottom and plain, colored T-shirts on top, each of us in a different color. We made two rows and we did half the song with Scarlett's row in front and half the song with my row in front.

The more we sang together, the more the merrier we were!

We practiced our ukulele part, and we practiced our singing part. We practiced looking out at the audience and smiling. We even practiced bowing.

On Wednesday after school, we had our Songwriting Club meeting and sang the whole thing for Ms. Adamson.

"It's wonderful," she said. "I'm so proud of you all for working together. I know it wasn't easy."

The show was coming up on Friday.

Some of us were tall. Some of us were short. Some of us had flat hair. Some of us had holes in our smiles, but we were ready!

Chapter Nineteen

ANTS IN OUR PANTS

On Friday we were so excited. The show was going to be during the last period of the day. While we were putting our ukes in our cubbies, we couldn't stop talking about it. We looked fantastic in our jeans and colorful T-shirts. Mine was orange! The color of happy! We were extra excited because families were invited. My dad, Mom, Leo, and Lily were coming. The whole flock!

"Boys and girls, you have ants in your pants!" Mrs. Brock said. "Does anyone know what a group of ants is called?"

"A colony!" Phillip said. "You're going to love our song for the show, Mrs. Brock. It has animal group names in it."

I started singing, *"A flock floating together is sweeter than swee—"*

"Lucy, it's time for our morning routine," Mrs. Brock said. "So please zip your lips."

"Zip your lips is a good rhyme, Mrs. Brock," I said. "It could be a song."

She smiled. "Not right now. Let's get our day started."

It was hard to focus, but we got through the morning. At recess we practiced again. Finally, last period arrived.

Then the principal made an announcement: "All performers for the show, please go to the gym."

We jumped up and got our ukuleles out of our cubbies and started walking toward the gym. Scarlett was going *clack, clack, clack* because she had on her fanciest shoes.

"Scarlett! Lucy!"

We turned around. Mrs. Tandy was walking up the hallway with a big bag. She waved at Scarlett and me to come over.

"Girls," she said. "I know how much you wanted real matching costumes. I got some cute tops and matching bobby pins at the last minute! Look!" She pulled out a package of bobby pins and four sparkly white jackets with pink flowers and fringe on the sleeves. Scarlett started jumping up and down. "Mom! I love you so much! These are amazing!"

My stomach started to get a bad feeling. "They're nice," I said. "But they don't fit the song. I think—"

"Pablo and Phillip can wear their T-shirts and stand in the back. The girls can wear these," Scarlett said, and tipped the bag upside down. It was empty. "Mom!" she said. "We need seven jackets."

"I thought it was you, Victoria, Mara, and Lucy," she said.

"No! There are seven girls in the Songwriting Club. There are us plus Resa, Saki, and Natalie." Scarlett's face looked like she was dying.

"I'm sorry, honey," Mrs. Tandy said.

"We should stick with our T-shirts," I said.

Scarlett stuffed the jackets and bobby pins in the bag

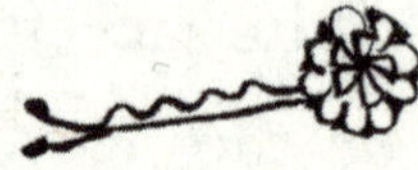

and ran ahead with it, her heels going *clack, clack, clack* again.

Mrs. Tandy huffed and walked away.

Phillip and Resa came over.

"What's going on?" Resa asked.

Phillip made a horrified face. "Did I see sparkly jackets? Really? I am not wearing one of those things."

"Don't worry," I said. "We can't use them. There's only four."

When we got to the gym, we all went crazy. Ms. Adamson had put up lights and set up a stage.

Scarlett called everybody over for a huddle.

"I have these amazing costumes," she said. "One for me, one for Mara, one for Victoria, and one for . . ." She looked around.

"Scarlett," I said. "We should all wear our regular shirts. We look great."

"But these are amazing!" She held one up.

"Let take a vote," Phillip said. "All in favor of wearing our T-shirts, raise your hand."

Phillip, Resa, Saki, Natalie, Pablo, and I all raised our hands. Scarlett, Victoria, and Mara were the only ones who wanted to wear the sparkly jackets.

Scarlett gave Victoria and Mara each a jacket. "Fine. *We'll* wear them."

"That won't look right," Resa said. "We won't look like a group."

Scarlett turned red. "Fine," she said. She put the jackets back in the bag and stood there, looking sad and mad. Then she pulled out the package of bobby pins. There were eight in the package. They were silver with a tiny glittery flower on the end. Scarlett gave each girl one bobby pin. "At least we can have a little sparkle in our hair," she said sadly.

Resa and I looked at each other. I could tell she was thinking how bossy Scarlett was being, but neither of us said anything. We took the bobby pins. Not everything is worth a fight.

Ms. Adamson called all the performers to stand by the stage. It was mostly fifth graders. There was a magic act, a comedy skit, a violin player, and a piano player. And then two fifth-grade girls who were doing a ballet dance walked in wearing costumes with sparkles, and I thought Scarlett was going to explode with jealousy.

"I should have done ballet!" she moaned.

Ms. Adamson talked us through the order of all the acts. The Songwriting Club had the most kids in it, so we were going to be last. The grand finale!

We looked good with our different-colored shirts and our ukuleles.

When the kids and families started coming in, Ms. Adamson took us all to the side hallway right outside the gym. "Wait out here," she said. "When it's time for your act to go on, I'll come and get you."

I peeked through the doorway as she was talking.

My family was walking in. This was going to be the best day of my life!

Chapter Twenty

CLEANING SUPPLIES AND A BIG SURPRISE

The show started! We all got nervous.

The ballet girls began practicing their dance in the hallway.

"Check out the way Scarlett is looking at those costumes," Phillip whispered. "Her eyes are woozy. The sparkles are hypnotizing her."

"She loves sparkles," I whispered back.

"Don't look, Scarlett," Victoria said. "It will make you crazy."

Scarlett turned away from the ballet dancers. "How about if I wear a sparkly jacket?"

Pablo rolled his eyes. "No way, Scarlett. We already agreed."

"Let's find a place to go over our song," Resa said.

We didn't want anybody to hear us, so we walked down the hallway looking for a place. Scarlett opened the door to the room with cleaning supplies. "This is nice and private," she said, and turned on the light.

Phillip, Resa, Pablo, Natalie, Saki, and I went in.

Victoria stopped. "Wait. I really have to go to the bathroom."

"Me too!" Mara said.

"Go quick," Saki said.

"I'm going, too," Scarlett said. "We'll be right back. Don't start without us."

The three of them left.

"Let's sing some of our other songs to warm up," Phillip said.

We closed the door so nobody would hear us. Then we started playing.

"Wait," Pablo said. He looked embarrassed. "I have to go to the bathroom, too." He tried to open the door. "I think it's locked," he said.

"It can't be true!" Phillip said. He jiggled the knob. It wouldn't move.

"We're locked in?" Resa asked.

Oh no! I tried turning the knob, too.

"This is bad!" Natalie said.

"Scarlett and Victoria and Mara will come," Saki said. "They can open the door from that side."

Just then we heard a sound . . . *clack, clack, clack* . . . Scarlett's shoes! She was coming!

I pounded on the door. "Hey, Scarlett! Let us out!"

There was silence. We all looked at the doorknob, expecting it to turn.

"They're locked in?" Mara's voice asked.

"Yes," Resa said. "We're locked in. Open the door."

Then we heard Scarlett whisper, "Let's go! We can wear the sparkly jackets and do the show! Come on!"

We were speechless.

Before we could say anything, we heard the horrible clacking of shoes running away.

No! We started pounding on the door.

Bam! Bam! Bam!

"Help! Let us out!" we cried.

Silence.

"I can't believe they would do this to us," Resa said.

"They can't get away with it," Saki said. "Ms. Adamson will notice we're not there. She'll stop the show."

Phillip shook his head. "Ms. Adamson always says, 'The show must go on!'"

"But Ms. Adamson will ask Scarlett where we are," Saki said.

"Knowing Scarlett, she'll lie!" I said. "She'll tell her we all chickened out."

"And then Ms. Adamson will say, 'The show must go on!'" Phillip said.

We all started pounding again.

Bam! Bam! Bam!

We called and called. Nobody answered.

There were no windows. Just a sink and some mops and brooms and lots of paper towels, toilet paper, and soap. We dragged a garbage can over to the door and banged on it with a broom to make more noise.

BAM! BAM! BAM!

Then we stopped and listened.

Silence.

"This is like a movie and we're in prison," Natalie said.

"It's Friday," Phillip said. "Everybody will go home after the show.

"Nobody will find us and we'll have to stay here all weekend and starve!" Natalie looked like she wanted to cry.

"We can chew on empty toilet paper rolls," I said. "Mr. Chomper would be in heaven."

Resa sat down. "Scarlett, Victoria, and Mara are probably putting on their sparkly jackets and getting ready to sing."

"They're going to sing our song," Phillip said.

"And everybody will love it and they won't even miss us because of all the sparkles in their eyes," I said. I pictured my mom and dad and Leo and Lily all watching Scarlett instead of me. "This is the saddest day of my life."

"We cannot miss this!" Pablo said.

"Yeah," Saki agreed. "We have to figure out a way to open the door."

Chapter Twenty-One

A LOCKED FLOCK!

When you are stuck in a locked room, it's easy to panic.

Phillip was chewing his fingernails.

Pablo was bouncing up and down.

Resa and Saki were pounding on the walls.

Natalie was sitting down with her head on her knees.

I was pacing.

An idea popped into my head. "We could stop up the sink with paper towels and turn on the water and let it flood out the door," I said. "Someone will see it."

"I don't know," Phillip said. "We'll get in trouble."

"We'll drown," Natalie said.

Another idea popped into my head. "We could dig our way through the floor and make a tunnel all the way to the gym."

Pablo held up a broom. "Dig our way out with this?"

He was right. We didn't have any digging tools.

"I have an idea," Resa said. She found a pen and wrote "Help! We're locked in!" on a paper towel and slipped it under the door.

We huddled near the door and listened. The hallway was silent.

"Nobody will see it," Natalie said. "All the teachers and kids are in the gym."

Then we heard a sound. Someone humming!

"It's Mr. Tapper!" Phillip said. "He's probably sweeping the hallway!"

Our school's custodian loves music. He always sweeps the hallway with his headphones on, listening to music and humming along.

The humming was getting louder! He was coming! He was going to see our note and rescue us!

Everybody started jumping and cheering. Phillip and I got down and peered under the crack below the door.

Suddenly, we could see Mr. Tapper's big mop swoosh right by the door. He swept up our Help note and just kept going!

We jumped up and shouted. "Wait! Come back!"

We waited and waited, but his headphones kept him from hearing us.

"He must have thought the note was a piece of trash," Pablo said.

"He should have noticed the writing on it!" Saki said.

Phillip shook his head. "You can't blame a guy for doing his job. He is one good cleaner-upper."

Our group was losing hope.

"We have to come up with another way out!" I said. "Come on, brain! Think! Think! Think!"

I tapped my head, and then . . . *plink!* My glittery bobby pin fell out and landed on the floor. I picked it up. "Hey!" I said. "On TV, people are always picking locks with bobby pins. Maybe *we* can!"

"Yes!" Phillip raised his fist. "Great idea!"

I stuck the bobby pin into the keyhole.

"Jiggle it around," Phillip said.

Jiggle. Jiggle.

"Try wiggling it more," Resa said.

Wiggle. Wiggle. Jiggle.

Everyone was watching me and holding their breath.

Jiggle. Wiggle. Jiggle. Wiggle.

"No pressure, Lucy," Saki said. "But this has to work!"

Jiggle. Wiggle. Jiggle. Wiggle. Wiggle. Wiggle.

"We're never getting out," Natalie said.

And then . . . *Jiggle. Jig—click!*

It opened!

Everybody jumped with joy.

Phillip took the bobby pin out of my hand and kissed it. "I never knew I would fall in love with a bobby pin. Thank you, thank you, glittery thing!"

We all laughed. Then we high-fived one another. *Woo-hoo!* Freedom! We grabbed our ukuleles and ran out.

Chapter Twenty-Two

WILL THE SHOW GO?

By the time we got to the doorway of the gym, Scarlett, Victoria, and Mara were walking onto the stage with their sparkly white jackets over their T-shirts.

"And now for the grand finale!" Ms. Adamson said. "Scarlett, where are the others?"

"Here we are!" I called.

We hurried in. Scarlett, Victoria, and Mara looked scared. They knew what they did was wrong.

"Should we tell and get them kicked out?" Resa whispered as we walked up.

"Later," Phillip said. "Right now, the show must go on."

With our ukuleles and our colorful T-shirts, the six of us stood in a line in front of the three girls. We were like two different groups.

I tried not to think about Scarlett. I looked out. There was my mom and dad and Leo and Lily smiling and waving.

"Move," Scarlett whispered, and tried to squeeze between Phillip and me. "Nobody can see us back here."

"We're in front because we're late!" I whispered back.

"Yeah," Phillip said. "Somehow we got locked in the supply room!"

Victoria and Mara looked embarrassed. "Sorry," I heard them both whisper.

"Scarlett made me do it," Mara whispered to Pablo.

Scarlett didn't say a word.

We started strumming. The audience was smiling and bobbing their heads to the beat. My heart was pounding, but in a happy way. It felt like a troop of tiny monkeys inside me was starting up the best party ever.

And then . . . just when we were about to sing . . . you will never believe what happened.

I guess Scarlett couldn't stand being in the back row. So she pushed her way between Phillip and me. And let me tell you, when Scarlett wants something, she goes all the way. She pushed so hard, she tripped over her fancy shoes. Her ukulele flew up in the air. . . . I caught it as Scarlett skidded to the edge!

"Aaaaaaaaaaaaack!" she screamed, and flapped her arms, and then . . . *thud.* She fell off the stage in front of the whole school. Fancy shoes, sparkly jacket, and all.

Scarlett's mom rushed to her, and Scarlett started crying.

Nobody laughed.

When somebody does something really embarrassing—even if they deserve it—you have to feel sorry for them.

Ms. Adamson wanted to make sure Scarlett's bones weren't broken, but Scarlett just wanted to get out of there. Her face was red, and she wouldn't look up.

"Can you perform, or do you want to leave?" Ms. Adamson whispered.

"Leave," Scarlett whispered back.

Mrs. Tandy put her arm around Scarlett, and they started walking out of the gym.

Quickly, Ms. Adamson turned to us. "The show must go on!" she said.

We all stood there in shock. In their sparkly jackets, Victoria and Mara looked like they wanted to crawl under a rock. I couldn't imagine them singing. And even though Scarlett had been so mean, she had come up with a great tune. It didn't feel right to perform like this. How could we sing joyfully when none of us felt joyful? I glanced at Phillip. I could tell he felt the same way.

I looked back out. Scarlett was almost at the door.

"Scarlett," I called.

She turned around.

"Come back!" I said.

She stood for a moment, blinking. Then she took off her sparkly jacket, threw it on the floor, and ran up to the stage with a big smile on her face. Victoria and Mara took off their sparkly jackets, too.

"Thank you, Lucy!" Scarlett whispered.

I faced the group. "Okay, let's get into two lines and switch halfway through so everybody gets a turn being in the front row. Just like we practiced."

We played and sang our song, and the audience went crazy.

The more we sing together,
The more we sing together,
The more the merrier we'll be!

Hooray! Woo-hoo!
Yippee!
The End,
by Lucy McGee.

THE SONGWRITING CLUB SONGS

Have fun with the songs in this book. You can hear the songs and sing along by going to the special Lucy page: www.maryamato.com/lucy-songs. You can also find out more about making up your own songs and learning how to play songs on ukulele, piano, or guitar.

THE TOGETHER SONG

(With extra words by Phillip!)

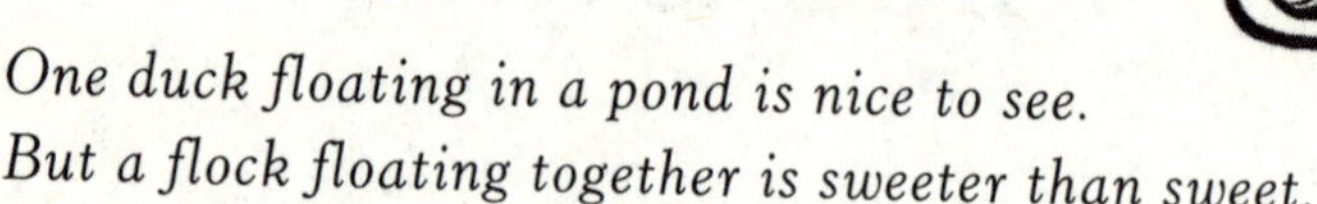

One duck floating in a pond is nice to see.
But a flock floating together is sweeter than sweet.

The more we float together,
the more we float together,
the more the merrier we'll be.

A lion roaming all alone might want to cry.
But if her friends all join her, she's got her pride.

The more we roam together,
the more we roam together,
the more the merrier we'll be.

A dolphin swimming solo is so odd.
But they have way more fun swimming in a pod.

The more we swim together,
the more we swim together,
the more the merrier we'll be.

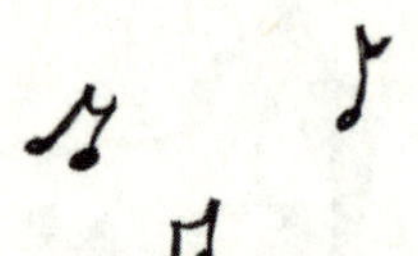

Fish love a school.
Horses love a team.
Wolves love a pack.
That's what they need.
Happy little clams
love a bed in the sea.
Everybody loves
good company.

Somehow you + you + me equals more than three.
'Cause when we sing together, we sing joyfully.

The more we sing together,
the more we sing together,
the more the merrier we'll be.

THE HOWL SONG

(Make sure to really let loose when you howl in this song!)

I want to stay in my closet
right now.
I want to stay in my closet
and howl.

Everyone will hear me
and say, "Wow, oh wow.
We feel sorry for that kid
in the closet."

Aawooo! Aawooo!

I want to stay in my closet
and howl.
Don't try and make me
come out.

Don't cheer me up,
'Cause I won't allow it.
Just feel sorry for the kid
in the closet.

Aawooo! Aawooo! Aawooo!

HAIR WITH FLAIR JINGLE

Is your hair a nightmare?
I care about hair! I repair hair! Oooh!
I dare to take the scare
right out of your hair! Oooh!
I'll turn it into hair with flair!
With your brand-new hair, I declare,
you'll feel like a millionaire!

WHEN I'M HOME

When I feel sad and shivery,
home is where I want to be.
That's where I know I belong—
Me and my family.

Oh, when I'm home . . .
Oh, when I'm home . . .
So much can happen in an ordinary day.
I know that when I'm home, I'll be okay.

Though our clothes are kind of worn out,
torn right where they shouldn't be,
And our hair's a mess . . .
Nothing fancy's fine with me.

Oh, when I'm home . . .
Oh, when I'm home . . .
So much can happen in an ordinary day.
I know that when I'm home, I'll be okay.

Inside jokes and made-up games
and noisy laugh-out-louds.
Sometimes we hug so hard
we knock each other down.

Home Sweet Home, Oh!
Home Sweet Home, Oh!
Home is where I want to go.
There I'll be okay.

Oh, when I'm home . . .
Oh, when I'm home . . .
So much can happen in an ordinary day.
I know that when I'm home, I'll be okay.

COMING SOON!

LUCKY ME, LUCY MCGEE

Read a sneak peek from Lucy's next adventure. . . .

Chapter One

"Mom!" I yelled. "Have you seen my uke?"

My mom tapped me on the shoulder. "I'm right behind you, Lucy. You don't have to yell."

"Sorry!" I hurried past her and looked behind the couch.

"Don't tell me you lost your ukulele," she said. "Remember what we talked about?"

I stopped.

Last month I lost my favorite hat. Last week I lost my homework. Last night I lost a library book. I said it was bad luck. My mom said it wasn't about luck, it was about paying attention. She had to say it three times because I wasn't paying attention. Then she said if I didn't get better at paying attention, she'd lose her mind.

I had to find my uke!

"It's probably in my room," I said. I smiled, even though I was worried. I had already looked in my bedroom. And in the bathroom. And in every other room in the house. No uke.

"Breakfast, Lucy!" my dad called from the kitchen. "It's almost time for school!"

My mom said good-bye and left for work.

"Keep an eye on Lily while you eat," my dad told me before he went to the basement to get a new sponge. I plopped down in my chair and ate a bite of cold toast. Lily sat in her high chair, stuck her fingers in the jelly jar, and then licked them.

"Lily, that's gross," I said, and moved the jar away. "Where did Leo go?"

She pointed under the table. "Tutta."

"Tutta" is Lily's word for turtle, which meant that my brother had turned himself into a turtle again.

I looked under the table. There he was all curled up, eyes closed.

"What's wrong with you?" I asked. Usually Leo turns himself into a turtle when he's sad or mad.

He didn't answer.

"I'm having a bad morning, too," I whispered. "I can't find my uke. Have you seen it, Leo? It's really important."

He squeezed his eyes tighter.

"It's going to be a terrible day," I whispered to Lily. "Why can't I lose things I don't like?" I peeked in the lunch bag on the table labeled LUCY MCGEE. "No potato chips! See? Dad put in zucchini sticks again! I hate zucchini. I wouldn't mind losing all the zucchini in the world!"

"Zuzu!" Lily said. She loves zucchini.

"I'm sorry. That was mean," I said. "I'm sure zucchini tries hard to be a good vegetable, and I shouldn't have dissed it." I leaned in and whispered, "I'm just sad because I lost my uke. Don't tell Dad!"

Lily smiled and then she reached out and patted me on the head with her gross, jelly-slimed hand. Yep, it was my lucky day.

• • • • • • • • • • • • • • •

"Lucy!" Phillip grabbed me as soon as I got to the blacktop, which is where we line up before school starts. Then he saw Resa and called her over. "Guys, guess who's coming to the Hamil Theater on Saturday?"

"The Queen of England?" Resa joked.

"Wrong," said Phillip.

"Aliens?" Resa asked.

"No!" Phillip said. "Be serious! They're playing a concert. I heard about it from Pablo. It's big news."

"I know!" Resa said. "Aliens playing ukuleles!"

"Okay," Phillip said with a smile. "I'd definitely want to see that." He pulled his uke out of his backpack. "Here's a hint." He started strumming a familiar tune. Resa pulled her uke out and started strumming with him. Seeing them play together made me feel even worse. I was ukeless.

Then Phillip started singing, "*After all these trips and falls, I'm gonna get up again . . .*"

"Get Up" was a Ben & Bree song. Ben & Bree are stars who sing and play ukulele all over the world. We watch their YouTube videos and try to play their songs in our Songwriting Club.

"Ben and Bree are coming?" I asked.

Phillip nodded and grinned and started singing their song again. That caught the attention of Scarlett, Victoria, and Mara, who ran over and started singing along. Everybody in our Songwriting Club loves Ben & Bree.

"Pablo said that Ben and Bree are doing a concert here on Saturday," Phillip told them. "We all have to ask our parents to get tickets."

Scarlett started jumping up and down, and then Victoria and then Mara. "I can't wait! I love them!"

"It would be so fun if everybody in our Songwriting Club went together," Resa said. "Don't Ben and Bree give away a free ukulele at the end of their shows?"

I couldn't believe my ears. "Did you just say they give away a ukulele?"

Phillip nodded. "They do it at every concert."